Sweet Dreams

THE BODLEY HEAD
LONDON

1 3 5 7 9 10 8 6 4 2

This edition copyright © The Bodley Head Children's Books 2001

First published in the United Kingdom 2001
by The Bodley Head Children's Books
Random House, 20 Vauxhall Bridge Road, London SW1V 2SA

Random House Australia (Pty) Limited
20 Alfred Street, Milsons Point, Sydney
New South Wales 2061, Australia

Random House New Zealand Limited
18 Poland Road, Glenfield
Auckland 10, New Zealand

Random House South Africa (Pty) Limited
Endulini, 5A Jubilee Road,
Parktown 2193, South Africa

THE RANDOM HOUSE GROUP Limited Reg. No 954009

www.randomhouse.co.uk

A CIP catalogue record for this book is available from the British Library

ISBN 0370 32763 2

Printed and bound in Singapore by Tien Wah Press (Pte) Ltd

CONTENTS

MY BLANKET IS BLUE

Hilda Offen

(WHISPER) *My blanket is soft,*
My blanket is blue.

When Mum says, "Sleep tight",
Do you know what I do?

I say to my friends,
"Are you ready to go?
Let's fly to the North
And play in the snow!"

With the moon to our left
And the stars to our right,
We fly through the sky –
We fly through the night!

My blanket is cuddly –

It's warmer than toast.

I can scare off the bears.
"Shoo, Bears! I'm a ghost!"

(WHISPER) *My blanket is soft,*
My blanket is blue.

"Let's go," says the cat.
"It's too cold for me!"

So we fly to the South
And swim in the sea.

I can lie in my hammock
Or sit in the shade.

I can play Bouncing Bears
And drink lemonade.

(WHISPER) *My blanket is soft,*
My blanket is blue.

I can stand on my head,

Ask a tiger to tea,

Tuck him up if he's ill.

So – Three Cheers for me!

We can ride on an elephant
Down to the bay

Where my boat will be waiting
To take us away.

We sail on the sea,
We sail through the night –

All the way to my room
Where Mum says, "Sleep tight!"

My friends sigh and yawn;
They snuggle down, too.

(WHISPER)   *My blanket is soft,*
My blanket is blue.

THE DREAMBEAST

John Richardson

Deep in a dark distant forest lives the Dreambeast. He sleeps in the morning, he plays snakes and ladders in the afternoon and he brings the children their dreams at night.

One day the Dreambeast couldn't sleep. He lost every game of snakes and ladders. "Bother!" he said, and grew very grumpy and cross.

"Bother!" he grumbled as he set off on his night rounds. "Bother," he called to the moon as he flew past.

That night he couldn't find any good dreams to put in little Tom's head.

First Tom dreamt that there was nothing to eat but cabbages...
and cabbages...
and more cabbages.

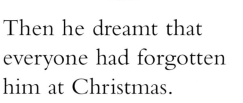

Then he dreamt that everyone had forgotten him at Christmas.

Next he dreamt a terrible blizzard blew his favourite teddy away!

Tom jumped up in bed and cried, "MUM!"

Mum came and kissed him better. She shook her fist at the night crying, "Naughty Dreambeast! You should be ashamed."

The Dreambeast was sorry for what he had done. He sat in his den feeling tired and sad, but *still* he couldn't sleep.

That night he went to Tom again.

Tom dreamt of a sad Dreambeast who couldn't sleep. In his dream he captured the beast and taught him his own bedtime secrets.

He shared his teddy and his mug of milk and his enormous comfy quilt. Then he read the Dreambeast a story.

Back in his den, the Dreambeast made a quilt of wool. He found his old teddy and boiled up a mug of milk with a little honey...

and slept and slept and slept and slept.

When he woke up he danced for joy.

That night Tom dreamt
of merry-go-rounds;
of candy sticks
and lollipops.

He dreamt that he flew through
clouds of blue, and over trees
with peaches and pears.

He dreamt of a
giant birthday cake
and of a party with
everyone there.

And he dreamt of that old Dreambeast
as he waved him a fond farewell.

THE MIDNIGHT FEAST

Lindsay Camp and Tony Ross

At bathtime, Alice whispered something to Freddie.

> What was that?

> Nothing.

> What is a midnight feast?

> Shhhh!

"Night night, love," said Mum, stretching to kiss Alice in the top bunk. "Night night, poppet," she said, bending to kiss Freddie in the bottom bunk.

As soon as Mum was gone, Alice climbed out of bed.

Come on, we've got to get ready.

She pulled the quilt off Freddie's bed and spread it on the floor. "That's for the beautiful princess to sit on."

What beautiful princess?

We must hurry, she'll be arriving soon.

Alice took a plastic bag from under the bunks and looked inside. "We need some more food. I don't think beautiful princesses like salt and vinegar crisps."

Freddie crept downstairs...

...and went to look for pomegranates and lobsters.
Mum was tidying the playroom and he didn't think she heard him.
When Freddie got back, Alice was sitting on his quilt.
She took the lobsters and pomegranates from him.

Alice wriggled a bit on Freddie's quilt. "I don't think beautiful princesses like sitting on ordinary quilts. We need a soft golden cushion. Go and find one."

Freddie crept downstairs...

...and went to hunt for a soft golden cushion.

A floorboard creaked, but Mum was in the kitchen now and she was humming to herself quite loudly.

When he got back, Alice was just making sure that one of the pomegranates was sweet enough.

Alice licked juice off her chin, and Freddie gave her the soft golden cushion.

Freddie hurried
downstairs, and
nearly tripped
over Beelzebub.
But Mum had
turned on the TV...

...so she didn't hear.

When Freddie got back, Alice was sitting on the soft golden
cushion, licking one of the lobsters.
The last one.

Alice took the enchanted musical box from him.

Is she still not here?

No...

...but it's very nearly midnight.

So, just sit down quietly,

and we'll wait for the beautiful princess to arrive.

Freddie sat down next to Alice...   ...and waited.

A few minutes passed.

Shall I go and look for some more pomegranates and lobsters before the beautiful princess comes?

It's all right. I don't think she'll be very hungry. And if she is, I suppose she could eat the salt and vinegar crisps.

Freddie waited some more.

"When will she come?" he yawned. "It must be midnight now."

But Alice didn't answer.

A little later, the door opened, and someone came in. She covered Alice with a quilt, and kissed her. She lifted Freddie gently into bed and covered him too. Then she kissed him. Freddie opened his eyes for a moment.

"I knew you'd come," he whispered, "my sister said so." And then Freddie closed his eyes and went back to sleep.

And dreamed all night of a beautiful princess
holding him in her arms.

COUNTING COWS

Dyan Sheldon and Wendy Smith

Dara can't sleep.

"When I can't sleep, I count sheep," says Dara's father.

"I don't want to count sheep," says Dara.

Her father looks at her. "Why not?" he asks.

"Because I don't like sheep," says Dara. "I like cows."

"Count cows then," says Dara's father.

Dara frowns. "But what colour are the cows?"

"Shut your eyes," says Dara's father. "Ready now?" Dara's father leans back in his chair. "Imagine it's a sunny day. A herd of brown cows is standing in a large green field. There's a fence around the field. The cows start to move towards the fence. One by one they begin to jump. Count them slowly, Dara. One...two...three..."

"What's wrong?" asks her father. "Aren't the brown cows moving?"

"Oh, the brown cows are moving all right," says Dara. "But the black-and-white cow is just lying on her side, gazing up at the sky."

"She's doing what?" asks Dara's father.

"I think she must be counting the clouds in the sky," says Dara.

"Let's begin again, shall we?" Dara's father makes himself comfortable. "Close your eyes," he says. "Tell me what you see."

Dara tells him. "I see a sunny day. I see a big green field. There's a fence around the field. I see a herd of cows. All of the cows are brown except the one that's black and white."

"And is the black-and-white cow moving?"

"Oh, yes," says Dara. "She's moving."

"Well that's good," says Dara's father.

"She's dancing around the field."

"Dancing around the field?"

Dara smiles. "Yes," she says. "I think it must be because the butterflies are tickling her so much."

"Now look here," says Dara's father sternly. "It's getting late. No more of this gazing at the clouds nonsense. No more being tickled by butterflies. Let's get ALL the cows over to the fence."

"I'll try," says Dara. She closes her eyes.

"What's happening?" asks her father.

"The cows are going to the fence."

"Even the black-and-white cow?" asks her father.

"Oh, yes," says Dara. "Of course she is. That's where the best flowers are."

Dara's father opens one eye. "What flowers?"

"The flowers that my cow is picking," says Dara.

"Picking?" repeats Dara's father. "Cows can't pick flowers."

"My cow can," says Dara. "She's picking them to put on her hat."

"Shall we start again?" Dara's father leans back in his chair and makes himself very very comfortable. "Shut your eyes."

Dara's eyes shut tight.

"Right," says Dara's father. "Your cow looks up and she sees the cows all running across the field. Is she looking up, Dara?"

"She's looking up."

"But not at the clouds," says Dara's father. "Or the butterflies. She stops picking flowers. She starts to run."

"You're right!" cries Dara. "She is starting to run."

"She's running to the fence!" shouts Dara's father.

"No, she's not," says Dara. "She's running to the tub."

Dara's father's eyes snap open. "What tub? There isn't any tub in this field."

"There is in my field," says Dara. "And my cow's taking a bath in it."

"A bath?"

"She's very hot," explains Dara. "Because it's such a sunny day. And such a very big field."

"Cows don't take baths," says Dara's father.

"My cows love to bathe," says Dara. "She likes the bubbles best."

"I'm closing my eyes," says Dara.

"Good," says her father. "And do you see the field? Do you see the cows?"

"Yes, I do," says Dara. "I see the cows and they're in the field."

"And what are they doing?"

"They're watching my cow."

"Because she's getting ready to jump over the fence?" asks Dara's father. He sounds hopeful.

"No," says Dara, "because she's swinging."

Dara's father looks at Dara. "She's swinging?"

"From a very big tree," says Dara. "She's drying herself off." Dara giggles. "She forgot to bring a towel."

Dara's father rubs his eyes. "Perhaps if your cow is dry now, we could try just one more time."

"All right," says Dara. She closes her eyes.

"All set?"

"All set," says Dara.

"Your cow has finished drying. She sees that the other cows are waiting for her. They know that she's the best jumper. They won't jump over the fence unless she goes first."

"I see them!" says Dara. "They're all in a line. They're waiting to go."

"And your cow doesn't want to hold them up," says Dara's father. "She's trotting across the field. Faster and faster...

Closer and closer...

Can you see her, Dara? Can you see her getting ready to jump?"

Dara says, "No."

"No?" Dara's father opens his eyes. Dara opens her eyes. "No."

"What do you mean 'No'? Why isn't she getting ready to jump?"

"Because she's looking over the fence," says Dara.

"At what?"

"At the ground," says Dara.

"Whatever for?" asks Dara's father.

"In case it's too far away," says Dara.

"She's not jumping off a cliff, you know," says Dara's father. "She's just jumping over a fence. Now close your eyes and really try to concentrate this time. Your cow is finally getting ready to jump," says Dara's father. "She's galloping across the field. The other cows are following her. Your cow picks up speed... She leaps into the air... Can you see her, Dara? Can you see her leaping?"

Dara's eyes are closed. She sees her cow. Her cow is galloping...
The other cows are right behind her... Dara's cow leaps into the air...
Dara's father begins to count softly.

"One..." he says.
"One..." says Dara.

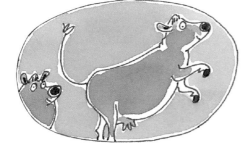

"Two..." he says.
"Two..." says Dara.

"Three..." he says.
"Three..." says Dara.

"Zzzz..." he snores.
"Four..." says Dara.

She tiptoes to the window.
"Five...six...seven...
eight...nine..."

SHADOWLAND
Nick Ward

One evening Lily went to bed early. She was hot and uncomfortable and couldn't eat her supper.

Mum brought her a glass of water. "Poor Lily," she said, feeling her brow. "You've got a temperature. Try to sleep for a little while."

Lily played shadow games on the wall. She made a rabbit and a butterfly. Then she made a swan, graceful and proud. When she moved her arm it glided across the wall as if on water; when she wriggled her fingers, it plucked and preened its feathers.

Sleepy now, Lily let her arm fall. But the swan was still there! It spread its wings and cried out. Shapes danced across the wall. A shadow moon rose up over a purple lake. Lily's wall became a shadow land.

Suddenly, the swan reared up and sped across the water.

"Don't go!" cried Lily.

A purple mist swamped Lily's room. Then her bed rose up off the floor and sailed through the wall.

Lily's swan was waiting for her.

The lake became a wild sea. The swan led her over the stormy waves and into a tunnel. Colours danced all around like dreams.

"Mum!" cried Lily. But her voice just echoed around the walls and then away.

Faster and faster they raced through the tunnel and out the other side.

The dream colours tumbled after them, making flowers and trees and sun and sky. Lily looked around in wonder. Shadowland was beautiful.

The lake was now a winding stream. The swan led Lily on until they came to an island. Her boat bumped against the grassy shore and she scrambled out. A path appeared in the bank and Lily began to climb. When she looked up, the swan was gone.

The island became a forest, cool and dark.
The further Lily walked the colder it got.
She shivered in her thin nightdress.
When she reached the heart of the forest,
shadowy figures, like little ghosts, came out from
behind the trees and then turned into real live
children. Lily knew they had been waiting for her.

The children joined hands
to keep each other warm.
Dark was falling and the trees
made long shadows across the forest
floor. All night long the children danced
in and out of the trees. They danced through
the night and into the dawn.

Then the forest was gone. Below them a sea of flowers rippled in the wind. Their heavy scent lifted the children into the air and tossed them gently about in the clouds. They flew up and up, right into the heavens.

After a while, Lily heard the flapping of wings and out of the clear, bright sky her swan appeared. He had come to take her home. The children flew after him, over hills and mountains and meadows. Lily's arms began to ache. Just as she thought she could go no further, they came to the purple lake. One by one the children fell from the sky and tumbled into the water.

Lily swam down and down until she reached the river bed. She watched the other children turn into silver fishes and dart away through the reeds.

Closing her eyes, Lily let the cool, gentle water wash over her. Her tired limbs felt suddenly light and strong. She spun herself round; a whirlpool caught her and pulled her up to the surface. She thought she could hear someone calling her.

"Lily," said Mum softly.

Lily opened her eyes. She was back in her room. Mum was sitting on her bed.

"You've had a fever," she said. "But it's over now."

Lily smiled.

Outside in the night, a swan swept across the moon as he headed for home... somewhere beyond the shadows.

THE MIDNIGHT DOLL

Maggie Glen

In the darkness of the corner
In its gloomy dusty darkness
Stands Susannah in a cupboard
In a cupboard never opened.

She is old and very fragile
Far too precious to be handled
Standing in her tattered satins
With her hair in matted tresses.

Long ago the one who made her
Made her for a children's playmate.
Oh, how sad they'd be to see her
Lonely, solemn-eyed and dreaming
In the cupboard's dusty darkness.

No small children – no more laughter
Just great-grandma slowly knitting
In the quiet by the fireside
With her needles and their clicking
And the tabby softly purring.

Now she sees someone is coming
Skipping, running up the pathway
And behind her comes her mother
Bringing flowers for great-grandma.

Oh, how long the grown-ups chatter
Long throughout the summer evening
Till the shadows grow like giants
Till the little girl grows restless.
And she wanders to the corner.

Now Susannah sees her looking
Looking, staring at the cupboard
Sees her climbing upwards to her
Feels those small warm hands around her.

Then great-grandma turns and sees her
Sees her lifting down Susannah
Sees her press her gently to her
Asking, "Was she yours, great-grandma?"
"Yes," great-grandma whispers softly.

"We must keep her in the cupboard
Though you love her just as I do.
She is old and very fragile
Far too precious to be handled
And we would not wish to harm her."

All too soon the front door closes
And the footstep sounds grow fainter.
Still and silent stands the cottage
Silent as the deepest forest.

Susannah once again is lonely
Sad and lonely in the cupboard
In its dusty gloomy darkness
Only spiders for companions
And the little woodworm beetles.

Deep inside her grows a longing
Grows a longing for a playmate
And Susannah in the cobwebs
Dreams a dream of great adventure.

And the tabby by the fireside
Eyes a-glowing like the embers
Sees the little doll Susannah
Make a knotted rope of ribbons.
Then, with small hands all a-tremble
Clinging to the silken sashes
She is slipping, sliding downwards.

By the door she stands and ponders
Ponders on the moon's great roundness
Sees the vastness of the dark sky
And its blackness pierced with starlight.
All the strangeness of the night-time
Fills the little doll with wonder.

All the little hidden creatures
Hidden deeply in the bushes
Hidden safely in the darkness
Call a shrill and sudden warning

Call, "Oh little doll run swiftly
Hide with us from Moon-faced Hunter
Hide with us among the shadows."

But too late she hears their warning
Hears the whirring of the wing beats
Feels the chill wind of their beating
Feels the talons close around her
Feels the great bird lift her skywards.

High above the park and houses
High above the very tree tops
Flies the fearsome midnight hunter
And Susannah flying with him.

Then she shouts and screams in anger
Screams, "Oh let me go, you monster!"
Screams until the owl is startled
And his deadly talons loosen.

Slowly downwards floats Susannah
Spinning like a leaf in autumn
Till her feet touch something softly
Till she nestles deep in ivy
That fringes round the lighted window.

Warm inside a child is sleeping
Dreaming dreams of times forgotten
Dreams of drowsy summer evenings
And of secret garden places.

Now Susannah with a tapping
Wakens up the little sleeper
Who, while yawning, turns and sees her
At the window, shyly peeping
Lets her in and holds her closely
Filled with happiness at meeting.

On the counterpane by moonlight
Midnight dancing, twirling, leaping
Warmth of far-off times returning
Such a happy, joyful feeling
Susannah and her new friend laughing
Dance and play instead of sleeping.

In the quiet of the sunrise
In the misty grey-blue morning
Comes the moment for returning.
Susannah climbing down the ivy
Hears her new friend softly whisper
"Come back soon, my little dancer."

Small, beneath the giant hedges
Swiftly through the dewy grasses
Susannah running, hurries homeward.

Safely back inside the cupboard
Damp with dewdrops stands Susannah
Stands as she has always stood there
But without a trace of sadness
Just a look that hints at laughter
And a smile that shares a secret
With the tabby by the fireside.

A LETTER TO GRANNY

Paul Rogers and John Prater

Lucy lay in her bed, in her room, in her house, in her street, and thought of the whole town spread out around her.

She fell asleep listening to night noises – distant cars and dogs barking into the dark – and thinking about tomorrow, when Granny would come.

The moment she woke, she knew something was different. Where had all the houses gone? The streets? The town? From her window she could see nothing but sea!

She ran out of the house, barefoot on to the sand – past the garden, past the garage, past the front door, under her own bedroom window.

"Breakfast's ready!" Mum called.

Lucy climbed back up the cliff, leaving a necklace of footprints around the island.

"The postman's late," said Dad.

"I expect the traffic's bad," said Mum.

"I'm going out to watch the whales," said Lucy.

That's where my school used to be, she thought, over there. This is where the road was. She picked up a starfish. "And there," she laughed, as two crabs scuttled away, "that's where Mr and Mrs Horner lived."

At lunchtime, Lucy told Mum and Dad all about the rock pools, the fish and the sea. But they didn't seem to be listening.

During pudding there was a knock at the door.

"I'll go!" Lucy said.

An enormous liner was anchored off the front garden. On the step stood its captain.

"Pardon me," he said. "I think we're lost. I can't work out where I am."

"This is 101 Acacia Road," said Lucy.

"Ah, thank you," said the captain. "Sorry to trouble you."

After lunch Lucy's parents worked in the garden.
"Look at these lupins!" complained Mum.

"Look at those dolphins!"
called Lucy from the beach.

Suddenly she remembered Granny.
How ever would she get here now?
Someone would have to tell her!
At her toes Lucy saw an old bottle.
She hurried indoors for pen and
paper and wrote:

Dear Granny,
I can't wait to see you.
Our new address is
101 Acacia Road Island.
Please come soon.
Love from Lucy

Then rolling the message up, she
slipped it into the bottle and
pushed it out to sea.

That was when Lucy felt the first drops of rain. The sky grew dark, the sea grew wild, and soon Lucy was hurrying to the house for shelter. From the window she watched the storm.

Now Granny will never make it, she thought.

Then, way out in the distance, she spotted a small boat. One moment it was riding a giant wave, the next it was lost from sight. But gradually it grew bigger and bigger until Lucy could make out her Granny, waving.

"Hello Granny!" she called, running to the water's edge as the rain stopped. Together they climbed the path to the house.

"You look a bit wet," said Dad. "Did you have to wait for the bus?"

After tea, Lucy took Granny
on a tour of the island.
She showed her the crabs
and gulls, the rock pools
and starfish.

"Look," said Granny,
"I've something for you.
Hold it to your ear.
What do you hear?"

So Lucy pressed the warm-coloured, soft-looking, cold, hard shell
to her ear. And in it she heard the sound of the sea.

Then she sat on Granny's lap, on the deckchair, on the beach, on
the island, and together they watched the ripe sun going down.

When it was time for Granny to go,
Lucy waved her goodbye from the
gate. She watched her climbing
into the boat and sailing slowly,
slowly away.

"Time for bed," said Dad.
"I expect Granny will steer by the stars," said Lucy.

That night, Lucy fell asleep listening
to the sighing of the sea and dreaming
all about...

...tomorrow.

LAND OF DREAMS
Michael Foreman

High in the mountains above the jungles, deserts and cities of the world lived an old man and a boy.

They lived in a valley of golden summers and silver streams. In winter everything was covered in a deep blanket of snow. In the higher slopes around the valley it was always winter.

Sometimes great winds blew through the mountains bringing snatches of song and slight traces of sound from the people far below.

The winds also brought fragments of their hopes and dreams, and in the cold mountain air these could just be seen – like breath on a frosty morning.

These fragments would be blown into snowy drifts and remain forever – unfinished dreams and lost hopes among the clouds.

But not quite forgotten. The old man and the boy loved to explore the drifts and uncover the dreams.

They would push and pull them into their valley, which became a vast store of bits and pieces. A scrapyard of dreams.

Sometimes pieces could be fitted together, and the old man and the boy would build and build. On warm days the entire collection would disappear, only to re-appear in the cold night air.

The old man and the boy worked well together, and between them could solve most of the puzzles.

When they had completed the shape of a dream they sent it sliding off down the mountain to the warmer air where it would become invisible once more and drift around the world and make people smile without knowing why.

Then one day a giant wandered into the valley. He was very sad.

"I've been a giant for a thousand years," he moaned to the old man and the boy. "In the old days it was great. I used to stomp about in the dreams of everyone. Now no one thinks of me. Earthquakes, thunder and natural disasters get all the credit."

"Can we be of any help?" asked the boy.

"No one can help a giant," said the giant with a great sigh that caused an avalanche at the end of the valley revealing more buried dreams.

"But you can be a big help to us," cried the old man. "Stay awhile and rest."

So the giant made himself a shelter from the rubble of dreams, and marvelled at the way it disappeared on warm sunny days but always returned to protect him from the cold.

After a while, the giant began to help his new friends with their work, taking some of the most interesting pieces of dream to embellish and extend his home.

With the giant's help, really big pieces could be recovered and assembled and sent off skidding and disappearing into the world.

Then, one day, they discovered that the top five hundred feet of the highest mountain was in fact the rubble of a massive dream.

There was no room in the valley for such a big dream, so they had to piece it together in the swirling mist and snow. It was so enormous they could not see the overall shape.

After many hours it was finished.

The boy, the old man, and the giant moved to one end of the dream and pushed. Slowly the dream began to move, then slid faster and faster.

Suddenly, the giant raced after the dream and leapt aboard.

The dream and the giant shot out of the mist and could be seen quite clearly before they vanished into the clouds below, the giant shouting joyfully, "Now they will remember me!"

The old man and the boy returned to their valley. The giant had found his dream.

"Perhaps, one day," said the old man, "you will find your dream, and follow it far from here."

"But I've *found* my dream," said the boy as the mountains slowly vanished in the warmth of his bed and he turned over smiling without knowing why.

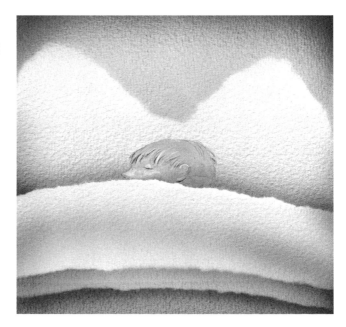

THE MAGPIE AND THE STAR

Stephen Lambert

This story began one night – when nights were not quite as they are now. Then, the moon shone full and round, all night and every night.

A time came, however, when the moon felt tired and decided to take a rest. Before doing so, she made a number of stars to shine in her place. The brightest star settled above a hill. Beneath the hill lived Pol.

Now, Pol was a solitary fellow. He lived by himself and for himself. He mistrusted the world outside, and although he had made a beautiful garden, a thick hedge ran around it so he alone could enjoy its fruits.

No visitors ever set foot inside – even the travelling folk somehow knew that in this place no welcome was to be had.

At night, Pol would watch the moon casting its light over his garden. One evening, however, he looked out and gasped in astonishment. The moon had vanished from the sky! In its place shone a single star. Its light touched the edge of the hill and its smile caught the corners of his mouth.

Pol felt in his heart that this brilliant star was a gift for him alone, and as time passed he began to love it and to treasure it above all things.

But Pol was not the only one to be captivated. From a tree high above the house, a magpie watched. He saw how Pol cherished the star and by his own greedy nature began to desire it for himself.

One night he flew down into the garden and spoke to Pol,

"I've a sparkling pile of treasure in my nest," he said. "Give me the star and it can all be yours."

"Off with you, magpie!" cried Pol, angrily. "All you see around you belongs to me, including the hill and the sky above."

"Well, what won't be given can be easily
taken," screeched the magpie and with
that he flew up into the black night,
seized the star and was gone!

Days passed. Pol began to mourn, and could neither eat nor sleep
for thinking of the star. Then, one morning, he made up his mind
to search for it. When he found it he would keep it for himself.

He set off at once, climbing the hill to meet the sky where the
star had once shone.

When he reached the top he found himself at the foot of an orange tree – its branches bowed over by the weight of countless oranges.

"Have you seen the magpie who stole the star?" demanded Pol.

The tree sighed. "I know that bird," it said, "for I heard it screech as it flew over. But my face was bent to the ground and where he flew I cannot tell. However, if you could only shake this fruit from my branches I will do what I can for you."

Pol hesitated, but he did as he was asked and when the last orange had fallen, the tree told Pol to break off one of its branches.

"This is my gift," said the orange tree. "It may be of use to you in your search."

Pol stepped on his way and after a while he came to a pool. Beside it was a heron, and drawing closer Pol saw that one of its wings was broken.

"Have you seen the magpie who stole the star?" he asked.

"I know that wicked bird," replied the heron. "But I cannot think while this wing gives me such pain. Two crows

came after my eggs and my wing was broken as I beat them off. If only you would help me, then I may be able to help you in return."

So Pol broke the branch and in a moment had made a splint which he gently bound to the bird's wing.

The heron thanked him, and from her nest she pulled a long, green reed which she gave to Pol. "This is my gift," she said, "and who knows, maybe it will help you find what you're looking for."

Pol followed the path until he came to a river. On the bank sat a fisherman with a net draped over his knees.

"Have you seen the magpie who stole the star?" asked Pol.

However the fisherman didn't seem to hear him. "What a day!" he sighed. "How can I possibly catch anything with this gaping hole in my net?"

"Take this," said Pol, and he handed him the long green reed. At once the fisherman threaded it through a wooden needle, and before you could say "Pike!" had mended his net. Then he put his hand in his pocket and took out a large swan mussel. Inside was a perfect pearl.

"This is my gift," said the fisherman. "Take it to the highest of those three hills you see in the distance; when night falls, lay it on the ground and wait. That greedy magpie will soon catch sight of it and be unable to resist. Be careful, though, do not give it up until he tells you where the star is to be found."

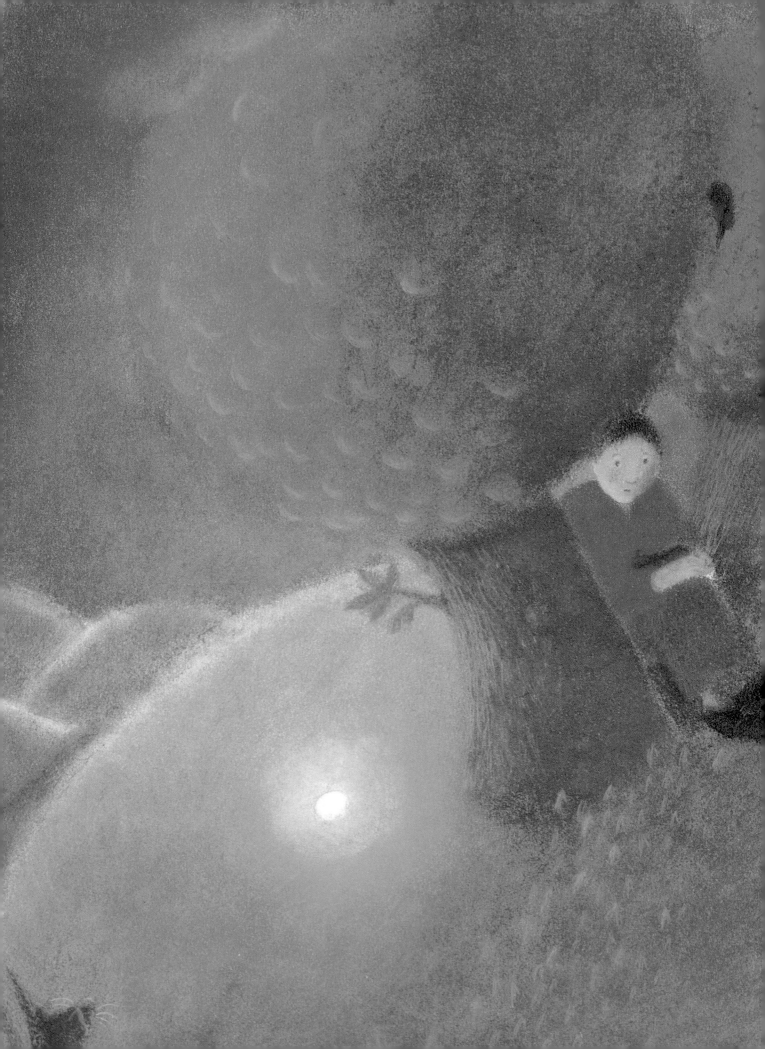

Pol was weary, but still he journeyed on – on and up to the top of the highest hill and there he placed the pearl. Then he hid behind a tree and waited until the sky grew dark.

Then, out of nowhere came the sudden beating of wings. Down swooped the magpie and made to snatch up the pearl.

"Not so fast!" cried Pol. "First you must tell me where you have hidden the star."

Now, the magpie badly wanted the pearl and thought how he could best make a bargain without really giving the secret away. He began:

"No hand can reach her though green fingers caress her. Hidden from view and curtained in blue. On a bed she lies but no blanket hides."

When the magpie had finished, Pol was obliged to hand over the pearl and the trickster flew off, greatly pleased with himself.

Pol tried to make sense of the riddle, but the day had been long and he soon fell asleep.

Whether they really came or if it was all in a dream, Pol never knew. But first he heard the fisherman speak to him:

"The star lies in water. The green fingers are the reeds that caress her."

Next he heard the heron:

"Look for the deepest pool in the river where the water is darkest blue and even I, with my long neck, cannot reach the bottom."

Lastly, from its hill far away, the whisper of the orange tree came to Pol:

"Remember how I was bowed over by the weight of my fruit? Well, fill your pockets with stones and they will carry you down to where the star lies hidden. When you have found her, empty your pockets and you will rise safely to the surface."

When Pol awoke he remembered all that he had heard, and set off to the river. He paused at every pool but all were too shallow. At last, he came to a pool so deep and so dark that below the surface he could see nothing but blackness.

Pol filled his pockets as the orange tree had told him and taking a deep breath, plunged into the water.

Down, down he sank,
a soft light guiding
him to the water's icy
depths. Suddenly, the
light grew brighter,
and there on the
river bed lay the star.
Pol's heart was filled
with joy.

Quickly, he picked
up the star, tumbled
the stones from his
pockets and rose
swiftly to the surface.

Pol stood on the river
bank and held the star
before him. Now, at
last, it was his to keep
forever. Then Pol
started. He thought
of the orange tree,
the heron and the
fisherman, and how
he had given and been
rewarded with kindness.

The star shone as if all the light of the moon was within it. Pol raised his arms and let it go. It soared up into the blue night, its luminous trail leaving behind a sweetly curved arc.

"This is *my* gift," said Pol.

Then he turned homewards, to his house and the garden that awaited him.

Above, in the sky, hung the star. It shone above the land below, over the orange tree, the heron and the fisherman, and over Pol.

THE GARDEN
Dyan Sheldon and Gary Blythe

Jenny found a stone while she was digging in the garden. It was dark and rough and came to a point. She had never seen anything quite like it before.

"Look at this," said Jenny. "I think it must be a magic stone."

Jenny's mother smiled. "That's not a magic stone. It's a flint." She touched it with her finger. "It might even be an arrowhead. It could be hundreds of years old."

Jenny looked around the garden. There were beds of flowers against the fence, and a fish pond in one corner. In the middle of the lawn there were a swing set and a barbecue. Beyond the garden there were houses and street lights and busy roads; and beyond them the stores of the town and the buildings of the city.

"What was it like here hundreds of years ago?" asked Jenny.

Her mother took the stone and turned it over in her hand.

"There were none of the things you see here now," she said.

Jenny stared beyond the garden, but it was hard to imagine what it must have been like when there were forests instead of cities, and fields instead of towns.

But then, far in the distance, Jenny saw a man on horseback, looking as though he might ride into the clouds. She blinked and the man disappeared.

Jenny turned back to her mother. "I thought I saw an Indian brave just then," she told her. "He was crossing the plains on his pony."

Jenny's mother handed her the piece of flint and they talked of how the world had been when the land was large and as open as the sky, of hunting on the plains and in the mountains and forests, of singing, and telling stories in the firelight.

"There's little left of that way of life now," her mother sighed.

"There's still my arrowhead," said Jenny.

"Yes," agreed her mother. "There's still your arrowhead."

Jenny stayed in the garden all afternoon. She tried to imagine people walking with their dogs and riding their horses across the faraway hills.

But all she saw were cars and trucks racing along the busy road.

She tried to picture young men hunting in the high grass of the plains, their movements slow and their weapons ready.

But all she saw was the cat stalking through the flowers and her mother's shrubs.

As dusk blurred the shapes in the garden, Jenny almost thought she heard women bent over their fires, their voices soft and laughing.

But it was only the radio in the house next door.

Jenny was still outside when the moon came up.

"Jenny!" called her mother from the house. "Come on in, it's getting dark."

But Jenny pretended not to hear. She wanted to stay where she was, watching in the garden.

Later, she asked if she could sleep in her tent, the way people used to. Jenny's mother sighed.

"All right," she said. "But we must put your tent close to the house so I can keep an eye on you."

Jenny lay awake for a long time that night. She listened for the howling of the wolves and gazed out at the stars. She stared at the sky so hard that she thought she saw a trail of clouds turn into buffalo and race across the moon. When finally she did fall asleep, the arrowhead was still fast in her hand.

Jenny had a dream. She dreamt that she woke in the night.
From somewhere close by came the murmur of low voices.

She cautiously opened the flap of her tent.
The world outside had changed.

The moon was corn-yellow and the stars sat low in a blue-black sky.

There were no houses or lights, no roads and no cars. Where the city had been there were only hills. Where the town had stood were fields of grass. Night birds called and the trees rustled. Jenny's garden was gone.

She looked around in wonder. There were ponies where the vegetable patch should have been, and dogs dozing where the flowers had grown. In place of the fish pond was a whispering stream. Instead of the swing set, painted tipis stood in a clearing, smoke drifting past them like clouds. And there, where the barbecue had been, a circle of people sat round a fire, their voices soft.

One of the men turned and looked towards Jenny. He beckoned her over.

Because it was a dream, Jenny knew what he wanted. He wanted her to return his stone.

The dogs began to bark as Jenny crawled from her tent, but because she was dreaming she wasn't afraid. She crossed to the fire.

The man moved over and Jenny sat down. She placed the arrowhead into his hand.

Jenny sat with the Indians all through the night, while the drum played, and the flute sounded, and they told her how the world had been, so long ago, when the land was large. When there were stories in the stars and songs in the sun. When every thing on earth had a voice and a heart, and time was measured by the changings of the moon.

In the morning, when Jenny really woke up, the world was as it always was again. The flowers were still growing along the fence. The cars were still speeding past on the busy road. The arrowhead was still in her hand.

Jenny stared beyond the yard. Clouds drifted past the sun like smoke. The beating of her heart recalled the drumming of her dream.

Without a sound, Jenny crept from her tent. At the edge of the garden she knelt in the grass, and buried the arrowhead back in the earth.

She looked up at the sky. And just for an instant, in the shimmering light, she saw the world as it once was, so long ago, when the land was large.

LULLABY
Shirley Hughes

Time for sleep, time to rest,
Snuggle in your woolly nest.
Let me safely tuck you in,
Dark without, warm within.

Far away, train whistles call,
Car lights sweep the nursery wall,
Muffled footsteps passing by,
A quiet moon in a quiet sky.

Soft blanket, smooth sheet,
Tuck the quilt around your feet,
Close your eyes and I will keep
A watch beside you while you sleep.

Acknowledgements

THE PUBLISHERS GRATEFULLY ACKNOWLEDGE PERMISSION TO REPRODUCE THE
FOLLOWING STORIES, WHICH ARE PUBLISHED IN LONGER, COMPLETE EDITIONS
BY ANDERSEN PRESS LTD, 20 VAUXHALL BRIDGE ROAD, LONDON SW1V 2SA:

The Midnight Feast © text Lindsay Camp 1996 © illustrations Tony Ross 1996

Land of Dreams © Michael Foreman 1982

THE PUBLISHERS GRATEFULLY ACKNOWLEDGE AUTHORS AND ILLUSTRATORS
OF BOOKS PUBLISHED UNDER THEIR OWN IMPRINTS AS FOLLOWS:

My Blanket is Blue, published by Hutchinson Children's Books,
© Hilda Offen 1998

The Dreambeast, published by Hutchinson Children's Books,
© John Richardson 1988

Counting Cows, published by Hutchinson Children's Books,
© text Dyan Sheldon 1994 © illustrations Wendy Smith 1994

Shadowland, published by Hutchinson Children's Books,
© Nick Ward 1993

The Midnight Doll, published by Hutchinson Children's Books,
© Maggie Glen 1996

A Letter to Granny, published by The Bodley Head,
© text Paul Rogers 1994 © illustrations John Prater 1994

The Magpie and the Star, published by Hutchinson Children's Books,
© Stephen Lambert 1991

The Garden, published by Hutchinson Children's Books,
© text Dyan Sheldon 1993 © illustrations Gary Blythe 1993

Lullaby, published by The Bodley Head in *Rhymes for Annie Rose*,
© Shirley Hughes 1995